my first visit to

the zoo

St. Anthony Park

English translation © Copyright 1990 by Barron's Educational Series, Inc.

© Parramón Ediciones, S.A.
First Edition, 1990
The title of the Spanish edition is *mi primera visita al zoo*

All inquiries should be addressed to:
Barron's Educational Series, Inc.
250 Wireless Boulevard
Hauppauge, New York 11788

Library of Congress Catalog Card No. 89-27246

International Standard Book No. 0-8120-4302-2

Library of Congress Cataloging-in-Publication Data

Parramón, José Mariá.
   [Mi primera visita al zoo. English]
   My first visit to the zoo/J.M. Parramón, G. Sales.—1st ed.
     p. cm.
   Translation of: Mi primera visita al zoo.
   Summary: Children visiting a zoo see bears, lions, tigers, zebras, deer, giraffes, and
other zoo animals. Includes information about functions.
   ISBN 0-8120-4302-2
   1. Zoo animals—Juvenile literature. 2. Zoos—Juvenile literature. [1. Zoo
animals. 2. Zoos] I. Sales, G. II. Title.
QL77.5.P37 1990   89-27246
590'.74'4—dc20   CIP
                        AC

Printed in Spain

3456 9960 9876543

my first visit to
the zoo

G. Sales

J.M. Parramón

BARRON'S

John, Mary, and Peter were at school one day when the teacher said, "Tomorrow we're going to the zoo."

The class arrived at the zoo just as it was opening. First they visited the bear's den. The bears had their very own pond.

"Look!" said Mary. "One of the bears is going for a swim."

The lions were nearby. The mother, called a lioness, was sleeping on a long, low branch. The father was stretching his big jaws to yawn. One of the little lion cubs was fast asleep, too.

The tigers were even bigger than the lions! One tiger was twitching its tail as it walked back and forth without stopping.

The deer had more space. They could jump and run around the trees of their little forest.

The zebras had lots of space, too.

"They look like horses with black and white stripes," said Mary.

"Look! Look! There are the giraffes!" said John. Their necks were so long that they could be seen from a great distance away.

The elephants were really big! One of them was throwing water over himself with his trunk.

Most of the hippos were floating peacefully in their lake. And then one of them opened his mouth. . . . It was huge!

The seals were really having a lot of fun as they splashed in and out of the water.

The kangaroos were jumping around on their strong hind legs.

"Look at the baby peeking out of its mother's pouch," exclaimed Mary.

The monkeys were climbing, running, swinging, and eating peanuts. They were the most fun to watch of all the animals.

"What a wonderful day!" all of the children agreed.

None of them would ever forget their *first visit to the zoo!*

MY FIRST VISIT TO THE ZOO

Zoological Collections

The first known zoological gardens were established by the Chinese emperor Wu-Wang in 1150 B.C. The later collections made by the Roman emperors included hundreds of lions, tigers, crocodiles, and panthers. But the Roman collections were used only to breed wild animals for the spectacles in the public circuses.

The kings and princes of the Middle Ages kept many different native and exotic specimens for the amusement of their courtiers. These collections aroused interest in the habits of wild animals. Louis XIV, whose zoological collection in Versailles was the biggest in the world, allowed some specimens to be used for scientific study and thus contributed to the development of modern zoology. After the French Revolution, many of the animals were transferred from Versailles to the Botanical Gardens in Paris. This zoo, which was also designed to help the study of natural history, was called the *Jardin des Plantes*. Founded in 1793, it still exists today.

The Modern Zoo

It was not until the beginning of the present century that the traditional notion of zoological gardens was transformed in a spectacular way. This occurred when a young German importer of wild animals, Karl Hagenbeck, suggested that the animals not be kept in small cages but instead be provided with habitats similar to their natural environment. These large enclosures would be surrounded by trenches that the animals would not be able to cross.

Almost all of the world's major cities now have zoological gardens. Among the biggest and most important are the Bronx Zoo in New York and the San Diego Zoo in California.

The Function of the Zoo

Zoos are basically designed to stimulate general knowledge and provide recreational outlets. But many of them also furnish study material for research carried out in scientific institutions at universities and museums. The zoos themselves also do important scientific research into animal behavior and play a major role in conserving species that are becoming extinct in the wild.

Friends of the Animals

The people who work in zoos carry out many different tasks, but they all have one common trait:

they are great friends of the animals. The keepers feed the animals and also keep them clean and well groomed. For example, they have to file down the rhinoceros's toenails so that the animal does not have difficulty walking, and elephants have to be washed every day so that their skin does not become too dry. Veterinarians look after the health of the animals in the zoo and take care of them when they fall ill. They even have to take care of the crocodile's teeth when the animal is suffering from a toothache! Finally, zoologists make sure that each species adapts properly to the zoo's environment.

The Zoo Menu

Wild animals in their own territory can hunt for their own food, but the animals kept in zoos have to be fed by their keepers. The keepers have to know what food each species eats, and in what quantities.

Each species in the zoo is fed its own special menu on its own special schedule. For example, lions, tigers, and jaguars do not eat every day in the wild, and therefore they are not fed every day in the zoo. The elephant consumes about 100 pounds (220 kg) of grain and fodder a day. There are also "exotic" dishes such as bamboo shoots for the panda, which does not eat any other food.

Zoos sometimes modify the animals' natural diets to ensure that they are nourished in a balanced way. The deer's diet, for example, is enriched with carrots, a food that the deer does not eat in the wild.

Sections of the Zoo

Zoos have special installations for certain species. The *terrarium*, for example, is where crocodiles and snakes are kept; there are special *aviaries* that are kept at a constant temperature for numerous species of tropical birds; *aquariums* contain various species of fish and other aquatic life; *dolphin pools* are used for shows with dolphins and sometimes include other animals such as killer sharks; finally, there are often *children's zoos* where children can touch and sometimes hold young tame animals.